I used to stand in a corner of the square at this time everyday to offer my condolence and love to my dead brother, Kai. I have to do it in silence without any flowers and candles. Everyday at this hour of evening. I know that some eyes are always on me watching.   They are deputed to.

I'm Shin Li, 45 years lives in Beijing and a doctorate in comparative literature from Peking University and presently an English teacher in Tsinghua. My husband is a surgeon in in the state hospital and our family is like other city families where fights and togetherness goes hand in hand and more precisely we lead more or less a decent life inside the four walls. Our kids are already grown-ups and doing their higher studies in UK. But my family is always worried about me of an awful reason which I couldn't shake off even if I had tried hundred thousand times. To my husband it could jeopardise my very existence one day even if they all surround me with all the protective shield they have. How could I deny my undefying relation with my brother, Kai killed in the Tinanmen Square Protests in the year 1989! I had a blood relation with him which is very close and that grew intense after his death. He became more alive to me after I understand him well much after his death, I was too young then when all that happened.

My husband knew all about it and everything to him as clear as daylight. I had not hidden anything from him. After we dated and engaged one day I told him : "Zao, would you be able to marry me after apprehending that I could be jailed or executed of being bloodily related with my brother ? The MSS are watching me all the time. They could put me in the dungeon on any pretext. Life would then become tough for you. They could implicate you also for me. " Hearing me with upright ears my fiancé or better to say my husband at present gave me a warm hug and whispered through my ears " We'll tell them to keep us in a single cell." Out of passion I kissed him with all my strength and we fucked for the first time.

My dad was a pharmacist and my mother a dedicated housewife who cared for everything in the house- animate and inanimate. My brother, a good student was studying engineering in the college and I was only seven or eight at that time, too young to understand the activities ouside. But the air is going to get hot and blow off any day- I heard those words when my brother was telling one of his friends. Kai was very sensitive to his studies and to everyone surrounded him. But I noticed that all of a sudden the number of bicycles parked outside our house got increasing day after day and friends of my brother began pouring in. I used to ask my mother " I'll also have so many friends when I'll be of my brother's age." Mom smiled at me and got herself busy in household chores. Outside the police patrolling began frequent in the roads, public squares and in the front of every government buildings – all that I saw while going to my school with my friends. It never occurred to my mind the changes happening so fast around us. To be frank, I was not so matured enough to sense those goings-on that could turn into a bloody massacre and that would lead to a perpetual loss to my family. I lost my brother in that most gruesome massacre which our leaders of the country have successfully covered up by fear tactics and severe brutality. Anyone at present time try to smoke it off or even try to talk about it in open would come under the strict surveillance of MSS who could cut him or her nicely without much noise.

Footsteps on the wooden stairs of our house became more and more thudding day after day and sometimes stamped on till midnight. People comes in and whisk off after having talks and gossips with my brother in closed door which sometimes blasted off and heard " This Communist regime should be replaced by democracy. They began surrounding us, scaring us with their machine guns and tankers, but we'll all see end to this." Eventually the combined voice, a bit louder to the earlier one spurted out , "Yes, yes, we'll". Often I asked my mother about all that's happening around which was not witnessed before, my mother used to say that my brother and his companions are trying to bring a new day in China that would be completely different from what we have now. Being a child of ten years I lacked such understandability

The only inanimate thing I adored at those days of my years was the bicycle- I used to take great care of it, a birthday gift from my father, pedalling for school and back home, short distances were easily covered by it and I considered it as one my of my best friends. At an essay writing in my class when I was asked to write down about my best friend, I referred my bicycle and described the movable metallic object with necessary subtlities that created squeaking laughter in the class. The ridicule shamed me for a while but I remain unfazed. Whenever something goes off wrong with my bicycle I took it to the nearest workshop for repair and fix it.

All of a sudden my father came home and told me not to take out the bicycle from the next day as the tension outside was mounting on. Authorities were barricading roads and lanes to put up a hard perimeter around Beijing against a probable riotous demonstration, the police were taking all the safety measures to resist any kind of disruption in the public life- all were prerequisities for stopping any klnd of unlawfulness, as they used to call that episode even now. It was evening when I was sipping down a hot soup and and my brother, Kai was not in the house, might have not returned from his college. Schools would remain closed and there should be heavy patrolling in the streets, even military was there in the streets to tackle any kind of worse situation. As far as I could recollect spring was almost over summer was approaching and the time would be the middle of May. The heat of the summer began burning our skin and beads of perspiration were surfacing on the foreheads, neck and armpits. Overexhaustion making us tired and sleepy but the turmoil outside was becoming grim and moving towards a flashpoint.

Near Muxidi students and people of pro-democracy wings had been on a hunger strike and the word hunger-strike didn't make inside me at that age. I asked my father out of curiosity "Papa, how could they strike the hunger? Are they really doing it?" Hearing me, my dad breathed out willi spilling laughter but after sometime soothed down my quest with elegance- "Shin, hunger strike means not to take food or any edible thing like fasting. And they are doing to turn the authorities to listen to them. You'll understand it when you'll grow up." Yes, it's true now I am old enough and wild too, to sense those words and the nasty inhuman operations carried out by the Army and the police against the people of their own country on that fateful day. It whirred out so fast and under strict control and surveillance that every demonstrating circles was nicely deterred and throttled.

I made to live in this country without my choice because I know that I would not be able to move out as the people of MSS is watching me round the clock. My every moves are monitored and even my family is closely surveilled. My brother died in 1989 massacre, i.e., about 30 years ago but I was still living a prisoner's life because of being sanguinolently related to my brother .Sometimes this thought ails me terribly- a crawling sensation run down through my spine forcing me to the point of no-return. "Why am I considered hostile to my country? Why am I being related to my brother who got killed in that massacre? Why am I always watched like a wrongdoer?" There are many whys piled up inside me which have no answers and at the end of the day – the unstained smile of my dead brother runs over my eyes which relieved me from those embittered whys.

Sometimes sudden fits carried me over and I was shrouded under a dense mist of ill-thoughts and suicidal urges, thanks to those Buddhist texts I read them– rescue me from the impending attacks , lead me towards a shining and glorious aura. The writings inside those texts aids me to get over those lonely crisis I seldom used to go through. Not being religious so but I go by the concept of godliness that emblazoned by truth and faith. Though my country has no state religion but to my knowledge there are many leaders and persons at the top of Communist Party lead a clandenstine religious life away from the eyes of their own watchdogs. I wrote an article on this subject titled "Believe in false beliefs" in my university magazine but was abruptly rejected on the filmy pretext of being too wordy. While being talked to the members of the magazine committee they had not offered me a good reason, even they fear to discuss with the issue like someone watching them from behind or from far like a sniper. In this country if you are noisy against the regime you're in a shit deep worse than the hell – there's no option for you to deal with either you've to go by the flow or keep yourself distant from all the misdeeds of the government. Injustice, forced labour, false trials leads to incarcerations are all the things that are rampant inside a closed watchful enclosure -even the wind dares to carry them out in the open.

I was threatened verbally a number of times and I was told if I try to make a noise about my brother's death or if try to do anything disgusting in their eyes the consequences would not be pleasing for me. My family was really upset with me about this and I always tried to keep my family away from this but I know that they could ride up to any heights or descend down to the downest causing physical and psychological inflictions to anyone related to me that forces me to confess that I've committed a crime or a sin beyond any doubts. Meanwhile I used to keep myself inside a non-vocal shell that helps me to pen down my thoughts in a diary that I keep in a hidden closet. One day I would like to get them published in some foreign publishing house when my children will be settled and my body would be immune to any kind of punishment even the scaring death.

That is the only prop of my life to live the days ahead, I really don't know whether I would be able to publish my dream book or I would be killed or silenced before my dream turns into realiiy. I don't know exactly what the people of MSS are planning or had already planned to do with me. Perhaps the worst I thought of. My husband and I had talked enough of this but could not reach into any well-founded solution. The only way to get relieved of all my worries- I used to go across the banks of river Hai and sat down by it, outpours all the tears upon the flowing waters.

My brother's death was really a sudden blow to our family. My father- a dauntless pro-democratic had managed to cope up with the death of his son considering it as a martyr's one but my mother remained inconsolable till her last breath which finally took away her sanity of mind. In a middle of a night in a mental asylum my mother breathed out for the last time and that was long after my father's death. A man who had the ability to enclose his sorrows and anguish into his heart with finest elegance had also succumbed to the misery rubbing his teary eyes in loneliness. I saw my father struggling every night inside the closed doors but he didn't lose his mind like my mother. The passing away of my brother and my mother's consequent insanity had weakened him from inside but he went on with his life hiding away his sorrows nicely under the flesh and blood till his end. He was also watched by the MSS but he didn't care or afraid of them. Donned with bravery he pissed them off silently and intelligently. His normal life had not been disturbed or damaged by the sadful events he had passed through. During those days my father was a bit dishevelled but it didn't last longer and I saw him how quickly he slipped into his habitual doings like a mechanical robot.

My mother used to cry almost everytime but her tears rained down profusely when she stood by the photo of my brother hung on the wall of our living room- smiling, ecstatic and freeness spun around him. Kai was there with my mother as she felt him almost everywhere surrounded by. The sorrow in her heart for her dead son could not be brought down in words but left alone to be felt only.

The day was almost cloudy when we were anxious at the doorway waiting for my brother but it looked morbidly strange- none of his friends frequenting our house came by. Only the sirens of the police cars and military vans were heard defeaning the eerie silence surrounded us. And my father was sure at " None will come, those who are alive had left the country or gone underground and the rest are dead or will be tortured till death. The Communist regime had even barred the foreign reporters and newsmakers from entering Beijing. They barricaded the entire city with every strength. They don't want to expose their brutality and cruelty -they don't want to show how they punish their own citizens. The uprising was subdued and throttled. If Kai is alive, we should be thankful or if never makes his way back then we've to assume he's no more. He's dead." My father could not resist his emotional outburst – banged the strong planks of the door with his furious fists.

A couple of days had passed off. I was not matured enough to understand what has happened and what was still going on around the city. But I was clear in one thing that something very bad had fretted through looking at the roads piled under burnt remains, fumes from them still emitting, blood stains almost in every pavements, few people who were hovering outside were under severe trauma and disoriented , empty shells of bullets lying on the asphalt tracks, army was still garnering – Beijing seemed to have been drowned into an abyss of obscurity. The animated pace of the city was lost replaced by a morbid skeletal ashen one. Only the undaunted Army was reigning wide across with fury glaring in their eyes. They were out to beat and kill everyone who were against the regime regardless of her or his age and sex. Like the merciless sun in the summer the Army was there to monitor, thwart and wipe out the democratic impressions. They were already done but seemed likely that they were yet to finish- they only crossed half the way.

We were almost sure that Kai was dead and waiting for the confirmation. Out of swelling distress my mother had ran out a couple of times but somehow my father had been able to turn her back like a reluctant child not willing to go to school. Years went by. She later dragged herself into a state of lunacy that took away her life wretchedly in the end. My father lived a life only for me and I was able to learn that while I was a bit older. I saw how my father had taken the place of my mother when she was almost out of her mind and had done those family things in great pains to keep the family tree alive. I also saw my father walking up and down inside his room like a rangy animal seeking shelter and comfort. It occurred seldom but I experienced those things so close that I had every reasons to hate the regime and to see the regime going down like other Communist regimes in the world. To see China in a democracy where every Chinese could talk freely and raise their voice against the wrongs of the regime is my only dream. But many of my colleagues and friends used to taunt my dream as hallucination which would never become true. But the words of Martin Luther King " I had a dream...." often rang into my ears that keeps my dream alive with me. Perhaps a day will come when Chinese people can make their choices freely, they can elect people to rule, they can also oust them if they think they're not good for them. They should not be scared of any authority while making demonstrations or revolts against the wrongs. My father died of cardiac arrest and I had not to witness his death since I was away from Beijing and in Shanghai with my scholarship. The news came to me while I was travelling in a city bus but I didn't cry out in spontaneity – I was shaken a little but I went straight to my hostel took off my baggage, boarded the train and headed towards Beijing to ritualise my father's last rites. While on his last rites I realised how my father had lived cowardly for me not doing anything but accepting his son's murder like other common events. It was a murder, a murder indeed committed by the state by the Communist regime as they did against all those who raised their voice for democracy during the June incidents. Heaving out deep sighs my father consoled himself by saying " You can't do anything against them, they've weapons in their hands, they've power, authority everything they have to put you down forever." He even advised me not to ruin my life running after my brother's death. And I also kept my anguish and qualms buried deep inside me in a secret closet. One day I will blow it off like bomber or perhaps a cracker that maybe louder or whisked away by the wind- but I will do it for the departed soul of my brother.

Three long years had passed after the expiry of my father and I kept my head down to the books completing my doctorate which would enable me for a decent livelihood. My fiance was at that time a professor in surgery and we met laughed exchanged pleasantries and often fucked . I find him a very well-behaved, suave and a practical man – not-so-good-looking but he has air of elegance around which makes him more charming. I never thought of marrying him because he didn't know anything about me nor do I but we both felt a strong inrush towards each other. Perhaps that entwined us both from inside and led us to marriage. Raising a family had never hit me in any way neither I thought about it deeply but I found it a rescue to my solitary living. I agreed upon my fiance's proposal and we married without any pre-conditions.

After a week passed I told my husband everything about the disaster my family had faced for my brother's revolt against the regime. He heard my untold story intently without breaking into the middle, not for a once. "It happened to every family of Beijing mostly."- he sighed out finally. Perhaps he was right miseries lies within the four walls of every domestic household just like us without any impressions. But I had never told my husband that I intend to do something for the departed soul of my brother which might help me to die without any moral pangs. Since I live in Beijing I often visit the bloody square and keep looking at the thoroughfare where foreign tourists often asked the guides about the incident and in response they keep themselves mum or say " It's censored. Please don't ask."

2

It was a rainy night. My father had just came back from his work and was preparing his tea as he used to. He lived alone and I took some days off from my studies and came to visit him. He was getting old but unfortunately there no one around to take care of him. So I used to come and visit him regularly which he also didn't like as he viewed that my visits could hamper my regular studies. But I never used to heed to his words in this matter particularly and he also knew that as well.

"How are your studies?"- He asked me while sipping the steaming tea.

"Its fine, papa. How's your health?" I enquired.

"Ok. Old age always has problems. If you're not busy, I'm going to tell you something."- his voice grew serious.

I turned back at him and told -"Not so, papa. Please tell."

"Do you want to know how your brother's life ended?"

His words pricked my ears hard and I closed the book in my hand putting all my attention to him. He looked up at me and continued the untold story.

" It was few days after June 4. The entire city was crippled under military crackdown but somehow I managed to go to Zao's house through lanes and bylanes, one of your brother's close friends to enquire about Kai's whereabouts. His father and his mother were also in complete distress like us waiting for their son's comeback. Zao's father was a bit strong took my hands and let me inside before I was rounded up by the military or by the police. Zao's father was a professor and an educated person but didn't approve Zao's ways of going against the administration. He differed angrily. He believed that the students, workers and the demonstrators were not united at all and they were ideologically disconnected and also didn't have proper plans to move ahead with their agenda or manifesto. What they planned was to dislodge the people who were in power and replace it by democratic system could not be possible with the way they had chosen. They hadn't made any dialogues with the government before demonstrating. They simply walked into the streets raised their voices which simply means going into a war without any artillery. Listening to his lecture I became bored and with a bit of discontent I asked him about his son and he cried down like a baby and he was sure that his son might have been killed in a pathetic way. It was his conjecture that the same thing would have happened to Kai also. To get rid of the throttle gripping over me I rushed out and on the streets again when I saw some military personnel a bit far away clobbering a young lad. The young man was crying wriggling and trying to stop them with his frail wounded hands but they kept on beating him until they put a bullet on his head. They fired at him like a mangy dog. Watching the horridness a dense cold sweat ran down over me which was about to choked me off but somehow I managed to get over and fled off from there. "

His voice grew feebler as if he could not speak further- his stony face spoke so. Quickly I ran upto him and offered my rescuing hand to make him feel better and tide over the hiccup. He rested down his head on my lap and tried to smile but tears replaced it like a sudden change in the weather. My eyes also became moistened and our sorrows for the first time walked together for sometime. It was evening - darkness had invaded through. Streets outside lit up and night came in a trolley of dark dresses. My father hadn't finished the story and he would tell me when he felt like-I thought so. He went to his room and I began to get into my books for the approaching semesters.

After a few days my father came up to me and I sensed from his gestures that he wanted to finish the remaining part of the tragedy. Closed my books and everything I had in my hand as I was upto to the edge of my nerves to know the tragic end of my brother. Helping my father who somehow straddled up in front of me and began from where he ended. I knew he had a good memory and he didn't need to be recollected.

"Within a few more days I could manage to rummage the entire city very carefully but unable to trace Kai or his whereabouts. And that made me more resolute and stubborn and I began exploring different many ways to get to him- alive or dead at the end of the day . It became tormenting for me as well since I became almost certain that he could not be alive since he had no means to leave this country. If he failed to flee he must have surely been killed by those butchers just like the boy I had saw while leaving his friend's house. Many of his friends were killed by that time and some were disappeared like Kai. Who knows where they were dumped or fled ? Sometimes igniting thoughts provoked me to snatch a machine gun from a soldier and killed one of them just they had killed those innocent souls like Kai. It was after a month long time when I heard from one of my colleagues that Kai was seen demonstrating at the northern flanks of Beijing on the fateful day before guns and bullets showered at them like pesticides. He also added that no one survived from that lashing fire. The demonstrators first thought rubber bullets sprayed on them to disperse but when they saw people falling upon over one another they ran amuck. But none survived from the deadly bullets. And all those news had made me more adamant in finding Kai's trace, might he be no more but as a father I had every right to see my son's mortal remains. Going to the authority would do no good or might become risky and the only way left was to ....". He could not finish the line, tears bathed down his wrinkled cheeks that melted away all his strength making him look helpless and miserable. I ran up to him to make him feel at ease rubbing his shoulders and back. Within a short time he got back himself into normalcy gulping down a glass of water and began with a firmer voice than before.

" After a week or so I heard that the government had been planning to bury a few hundred dead bodies clandenstinely in the outskirts. Away from the eyes of the common people. Perhaps in darkness during midnight hours. I began using all my connections to get every piece of information on this. And nothing of all these things I told to your mother as you could sense why. When I was at all my mind to get towards my son presumably dead the police and the military started punishing those families who were trying to trace the infidels- they began to call them in that way because the government was in a run to save the damage already been done in kiiling hundreds of innocent unarmed demonstrators and students. Kin Lai one of your brothers friend living a few yards away from here was also missing after that day and his parents made a collective gesture of protesting in a silent way. They stood in the square at the dead end of a night with a photo of his son and a candle beside him to show their outrage. But within a short while the police came and dragged them away from there ruthlessly to somewhere from where they didn't came back. This news hovered all over the city and the same thing inflicted to everyone who tried to embarrass the government in any manner they felt right. And those things were happening so fast that it began to scare me and sometimes I thought of withdrawing myself from my pursuit. I had responsibility for you and for your mother, too. If anything happens to me the family which was in misery would be completely crippled and then wiped out without any trace. Dreadful thoughts begun threatening me like nightmares. But in some corner of my mind a string of hope hungs surreptiously that makes me moving towards my resolve. Lot of things happening so fast and so horribly that families who lost their sons, daughters, sisters and brothers were distancing themselves of being getting caught by the police as the military and the police started defaming them as infidel families. Reports were coming to me from different corners that the parents or the members of such and such family were taken away by the police and went missing and those who returned dared to speak out in the open of the tragedy as well as the torture they faced and suffered. But I know in our locality there were many young people went missing after that incident but none had the courage to tell or to discuss about it. They just forgotten their missing family member like a visiting stranger- perhaps they could but how it was possible for me. How could I forget my boy whom I beget ? But it was so complicated that sometimes my urge compromises with my logics. A week had already passed. The tough policing and militarising was slackened and I got the information. A mass burial would be coming up in the outskirts- a few kilometres away from the airport. The place was almost vacant with some scattered foliage and was perfectly chosen for underground work. Living in a country where leaders speak about lofty ideals of socialism and sad to say they were making preparations to dump dead bodies of their own young citizens. However, I made a plan to make a survey of the place where the graveyard would be dug and the task would not be smooth enough when the prevailing condition at outside is so tense and volatile. But to go there which is close to the present day airport area and about thirty kilometres from here was a risky adventure as the police and military were still making frequent patrols. Besides that, public transport was not in the streets. The government has tightened its grip everywhere around Beijing as well as also in other parts. Imprisoning anyone whom they believe suspicious or chaotic. The police and the military were ordered to nab any person appearing destructive or hostile to them after the demonstration. Even the parents or the near ones of the killed or disappeared men and women tried to do anything as a mark of protest considered as an outrage. They were sent to jail or killed secretly- these were all government sponsored killings that could not be called for any justice. Travelling a long distance of about thirty kilometres or more seemed to become impossible for me since the military and the police had crowded up the streets and I had to make it fast since the information passed on to me was from a very authentic source. The communicator had also informed me that the military personnel were very much onto the diposal of those bodies as they started decaying and many of them already decomposed. The morgues had been full and place for keeping those bodies was scant as the numbers crossed more than five hundred only in Beijing. Can you imagine how ruthless a government be ? Killed people and then dumped their dead remains without even handing over the dead bodies to their families. This was where we lived - a socialist communist nation. A sense of overtemptness has rubbed all over me. Bravely I went out disregarding your mother's cautions to get to that place where Kai be possibly dumped. I wanted to see him for the last time. "

I saw my father was in a non-stop mood and was eager to tell me out everything and I didn't want to interrupt him either. Became   an unbothered listener I suffered a lot going through it but I was resilient. My father started again gulping down a glass full of water.
" I had skipped plan of making a survey of the place and decided to go on the day of burial. There was a binocular your brother used to carry on outings and I wanted to make use of it. If I get near to the burial place I might get caught and every harm would then be inflicted upon me. Rather I would stay away from a few yards of the spot and watch everything through that instrument. But I had no plans of getting there which was about as I said earlier eighteen miles from here. I was simply looking through the blinds and sometimes rushing out to see if the patrolling had slowed down. Hours were left to make a rash decision which I had to. But something was pulling me from back and you could easily understand that. It came to me as a boon the administration had lifted the patrolling for some hours and that was what I was waiting for. I was planning of whisking off from the house and took to the streets during those unpatrolled hours. Those off hours were between nine in the morning and six in the evening. I had a plan to work out. I wore a tattered shoe a half-torn shirt and a dirty pyjamas which help me to look like a destitute or a beggar and I told your mother to be off for a day or two. It was drizzling and the darkness of the clouds standstilled everywhere and I left the house after a goodbye to your mom. She understood but didn't stop me which was readable from her vivid eyes. I went out and the streets were almost empty except some dogs in the lanes running berserk. Quietly I took the main street and began walking like a beggar marching forward without any destination. My hair was unkempt every loose ends had fallen down covering my face my nails were full of dirt my legs much like that of my nails. I had stained myself with dust and ashes as much as I could before leaving the house to get a look of a beggar or a vagrant. You didn't know all these things because you're too little at that time. I want to smoke."
        I stood up went upto the table and handed him a pack of cigarettes which I used.

   " Take this papa. " I lit up his smoke and he fagged in the first one deeply and puffed out slowly making it a white snake in the air. Then he smiled at me and began the talking.

   " You're using this brand. It's good one. I had walked over four miles and it's still dark. The first patrol I saw after making through the lanes and bylanes came up to me all of a sudden like a thunder that shook me up and down. But I remain unnerved and kept on walking without looking them at their eyes. One of the soldiers walked forward and asked me – where was I going ? Lifted up my face I raised my finger and pointed it towards his nose, seeing this the other soliders lauged aloud in a chorus. Then they left me passing out some words- Mad, old haggard sort of. I kept on walking towards my destination. I was happy to myself since the trick had been playing. But the fear of getting caught and even jailed was also with me. Whatever might come upto I would not be deterred and kept on going till I catch the glimpse of Kai- my dead son. Wouldn't you find it grievous enough for a father to embroiled into such a misery ? But that's my destiny my very ill-luck. After walking over another five miles the sun above had came out feebly and drizzle by then had stopped. I was thirsty and a bottle of water there in my rugpack slung over my shoulder had soothed me down. There was some bread and a can of soup prepared and handed me by your mother before I left the house. After walking off some miles I sat down by the side of the empty road and broke a few crumbs since I knew I would have to go with this little provision till evening. I had money but if I went to a hotel or a restaurant for food eyes would fall on me and that could destroy everything I had in my mind. So I had carried on cautiously before anything goes wrong or out of my way. A person walks for his health and I was walking for my dead son to see his corpse. Sometimes while on the way my head turns into a red charcoal and tempts me to kill the police and military who were responsible for killing my son. During those walking hours every sensible and insensible thoughts crowding up inside me making me destructive at once . When the sun was almost overhead I felt tired and looked for a shelter to get some rest. Because I was only fifteen kilometres away from my desired place. So I took a little nap by the side of the road under an oak tree probably. The tree had a comfortable shade beneath and I sat down cosily under it with my legs extended forward and slowly I died down to sleep. More than an hour gone I was sleeping and suddenly a chaotic giggle shook me up. A dozen kids all were boys surrounded me staring with their immaculate eyes and laughing noisily. They took me as a lunatic looking at my tattered and dirty clothes. But I remain unperturbed and smiled at them which stopped

their laugh. They stood around me and watching me like an ape in a zoo. I loved their glances and after sometime carried on with my walking again. I started walking again leaving them behind with a lot of smiles because I had to be closer to the spot before the daybreak. When the sun was about to go down beyond the horizon I was almost at the close to the spot. But what I saw was really unimaginable. The place was already cleared and a large hole was dug which could be able to pile up more than two hundred corpses. I was really horrified to see that vile pit and at the same time shamed of being a citizen of this country. Since I was watching all from an elevated ground through the binocular which was unblurredly and clearly hitting my eyes. Evening had fallen and the sky darkened above. A downpour was imminent again and I had to drench all the night since there was neither shade nor any canopy to shield my head from rain.The military as well as the police cars and vans had arrived near the pit and the place had already lit up by the headlights of those vehicles. I was in a crawling state like a reptile with my binocular on my eyes. About an hour passed a vehicle larger than a truck arrived with dead bodies. The military and the police scudded the area like snipers and I slowly crawled back down where their searchlights didn't trace me. As soon as the lights were put down I crawled back upwards again to where I was and sighted the horrific thing I ever seen. They began dumping the bodies inside the pit like dead dogs and cats and every police and military manning there had scarfed their noses with handkerchiefs which tells those bodies they were dumping had began decomposing or already been decomposed. The corpses were off-loaded so quickly from the truck that I couldn't locate the face of Kai. It was all Kais dumping into the pit – I felt that way as my vision from that elevation viewed likewise. Journeying upto there for my son had made me somewhat selfish, my son had not only been killed there were a lot of Chinese boys shot and killed, even their parents had no information of them so to me I became a proud father of those innocent young victims or you could say martyrs.Yes, my journey to my dead son oh sorry to my dead sons ends here. I came back from there safely without a scratch and narrated the story to your mother who understood but keep on asking me in a bickering way – So, you didn't find Kai. I failed to lead her into my path of thinking and as a result overthinking of Kai drove her to insanity. It's my fault that I couldn't protect your mother, I took the responsibility. I failed to offer the calmness she needed during those overwrought times."
He kept quiet and calm and I was already oversoaked in sorrow and misery. The tears in my eyes had been flowing out and I looked up at my father's eyes which were also dripping down tears. He began crying like a

child- pulling out of myself from misery I hurried up and offered him a soothing stroke of my hands over his wrinkled face and balded head. We subdued each other in the most affectionate embrace that a daughter could only expect from his father or a father could only offer to his dearest daughter in such times. That warmest touch of affection could make thousand miseries melt away.

Two to three days left to get back to Peking since my exams were fast approaching. But I was leaving with an overburdened soul wounded by the story of a massacre that surfaced in my country where my borther was killed like a stray animal and dumped secretly into an unknown pit. I didn't know whether taking away lives by the government whom our lives depend upon was an act of crime or be termed as an austere measure. Lives cannot be crushed on any excuse be it a governmental misgiving or a mass genocide. But here there are many Tiananmen Mothers' who are still afraid to speak out in public of their miseries and lamentations. It is all censored. How can a government censor a mother's breastbeating on the death of his son whom she lost at his green age! It's censored because the government is afraid of facing the consequences of the killings of people. Could any mother in the world remain unmourned after the death of his only son? Could any mother be reticent when she find her young innocent kid was killed mercilessly? But to my mother the mourning crept in seated deeply inside her, battered her, crushed her emptied her and made her dismal before everyone.

On a late afternoon while I was back from my high school I found my father at home in a tizzy which was unusual to me since he used to come back after the evening fall. A neighbour called up my dad on emergency to rescue my mother who was running wayward in a demented manner. Neighbours knew about my mother's mental state but this time she was found almost naked in the lane shouting out "Kai, Kai...." repeatedly as he was looking out for him crazily. The grief heaped up inside her grew enormous and that had completely subsided her normalcy. Day after day she became violent and furious even to us who gets closer to comfort her from frenzy state. It was from that day our miseries and helplessness manifolded and that went beyond the limits of our oversit. I saw often my father sat in his chair with hands covered his face struggling all alone without any prop. Looking up at me sometimes in dishevelled eyes I ran away from there not to further his worries and miseries as I find no other immediate wayout. Her continuous lamentations took deep delve into her psyche exploited her damaging it slowly in front of my lucid eyes which intensified more during the absence of my father who remained out of Beijing mostly on work. Consequently as a teenager I had to face the entire brunt of my mother's disorientations and mental sickness which sometimes tempted me to flee from the house but some invisible pull set me back to my place. Initially she used to wail and talk alone in front of Kai's photo which lasted for some minutes and then it lingered for hours and then after some months when her wailings became almost unstoppable. It stopped only when she was exhausted and dropped down to sleep. Since our house was a big one we could easily manage to lock her into a room which was away from mine to avoid noise that was not helpful for my studies. When I was stepping to move into the college one day my father came into my room all of a sudden and told me that he decided to shift my mother into the nearest asylum. She would be shifted the next morning. The decision slapped me hard of not seeing my mother any more in the house where she nursed me, fed me, pampered me and governed me with all motherly care. The decision to sancturise my mother was also logical and reasonable as it was getting harder for us to manage my mother's insane activities that became more and more uncontrollable. We were under deep pressure in this matter as my father who was about to retire had already devoted one-third of his life in taking care of his insane wife, precisely after Tiananmen massacre. Looking at a glance anyone can find how tired and wasted away he was- the thick dark circular patch around his eyes, the bulging neckline, protruding ribs on his chest, nerves sticking out from hands, weary footfalls- all those marks made him a tortured man.

Perhaps the upheaval in 1989 has left no marks or impressions in the young minds at present. But the bloodshed carried out the genocide perpetrated could not get wiped out like the dust heaped on the blinds. Could the history of massacre be replaced by the modern digital Chinese euphoria? To me, it would never be possible whatever way the government pursue to make it a closed chapter. A crime should always remain a crime and it cannot be washed away by any act of goodness or charity. Never and never could it be possible.

My brother died and we couldn't even see his dead body and the misery that follows after his heinous death suffered by us would have to be carried on till all the leaves of our family tree withered away and died. Misery mulitiplies misery- there's a saying and it persists starkly in my life. My father, a humble Chinese had to live with the death of his son miserably and my mother had become insane miserably after the death of his son till both of them died with a brunted soul. So in my family miseries clung hard and deep inside us that more we tried to shed it off the more it became clammy.

Autumn was on the way surrounding us everywhere. Trees were overgreened and flowers such as plum blossoms, peonies, camelias looked spiritual in full bloom. Winter was yet to pounch upon its cold paw on us but we stood with all might to welcome the frigid spectre. Soon there would be whiteness all around in our rooftops, balconies, roads, lanes, in our clothes, hats and upon our eyelids. In winter China thudded like a dragon that creeps and stays with pain and pleasure. But to us autumn didn't have a pleasing experience. A bad news arrived but it was not unexpected at all. We lost another of our family members- my mother. In the asylum she breathed out last with her anger, cries, frustrations and also with an unquiet heart. Therapies and medicines could not be able to bring her sanity back since Kai had unmade her so badly. We hoped and hoped keeping our fingers crossed in getting her see cheerful and livid. But that didn't happen and when she died alone in that asylum we took her death as a salvation from misery. It was an unceremonious death truly that put an end to our visits to her which had became a routine exercise to us. Besides that, it also strengthened me to do something which my brother Kai had failed to do. But I didn't know what to do and the consequence of any misadventure could cost my life. Being a mother of two kids and a wife of a loving husband I had some moral responsibilities like my father but I didn't want to live like him prioritising the family ahead of everything.

My fiancé and now my husband used to scold me for not having a mobile phone and he always insisted me to have one for fast communicating which he to his thinking – the call of the day. But I don't like to have numbers to remember and to transport my likes, dislikes, wishes, logics everything that I was entwined with. Rather I prefer to carry memories that could mystify me, wake me up from deep slumber, hammered me like a iron rod, take me way down to the place I left decades ago. Memories that I only wish to live with. Some like green cabbages, some became brown nuts and some shapes like withered leaves yet to be decayed. Robustly I don't feel the need of social media to exhibit my miseries or my celebrations. Better I would share everything with my close ones who are closer to me always.

Vacation began and I was in my home with my books and provoking thoughts. Thoughts that always tempt me to do something which could stumble or could shake the government at least for a minute. Leaders of the Communist Party would have to shame their faces down for the bloody past- that's what I wanted to do. Silence couldn't be a revolution at all, I learnt that from my dead brother. Visits to the square had become a regular exercise to me, looking at the foreigners who were continually asking the guides about the tragedy but the fearful guides ignore them politely and switch on to other talks. Years gone the government was still so nervous about it that the people of MSS keep a close watch on the square. People who were earlier tried to do something obituarily as a mark of respect towards those who were martyred in the tragedy were carried away forcibly and swiftly from the square and then imprisoned or killed later. It means that the government was still sceptical about it's reputation in this matter and feared to take any chances.   The consequences would also be same if I tried to do something for my dead brother but I had to take the risk disregarding of what comes about.

It was midnight. Sitting on the bed with a smoke between my lips I was watching my husband lying naked who fucked me an hour before were sleeping tight. After a while I dressed up quickly left the room without much noise. Walking down the street I came up to the square and found it almost empty. I had a plan which I had to execute before my vacation ends. During those days I had knocked every newspaper office for placing a missing advertisement but everyone turned me out after reading the contents of the ad. The people in some newspaper office had advised me to give up my plans because a person who went missing for thirty years or more could be considered as dead. The ad was about my brother Kai who must have been died in the Tiananmen Square massacre like other martyrs but the body has not been found and so he was simply missing since then. It was a missing person's ad. Expected it would be like that it didn't surprise me rather I decided to go all by own. I had printed about hundred copies of the ad from my computer and stacked it secretly behind my bookshelf. If my husband discovered it he should never allow me to make it public the way I intended and that could bring about a domestic combat which I did not want either. Kai was my brother and why should I put my husband and my kids into such fray.

It was night when slipped out of my bed. With the printed copies and a roll of cellotape I began affixing the copies on every walls, lightposts on every space where they could be pasted. Fortunately I was not deterred or stopped by anyone but I knew the possible consequences of such act. The CCTV cameras everwhere around the square should have already captured my doings. I had completed the task within an hour and slipped back to my husband's side where he was still asleep.

I was awakened by my husband who was looking at me with his scary eyes and I hugged him down to me and told me " Don't do anything for me. I would not plead guilty." There were footsteps thudding outside the doors of my house and I knew who they were and what they came for. I dressed up nicely and greeted them inside. But the officer had told me that they had a warrant against my name and I had to go with them. Without furthering the conversation I abided by and went out with them looking back for once, when I saw my husband looking at me helplessly. I flashed a smile at him and went inside the dark van.

I don't know where I am now. But the place where I am dungeoned or more precisely imprisoned is solitary which helped me to speak to myself and to do whatever I feel like. But I don't felt miserable or repentant of what I had done. There was no remorse in my heart for what I had done for my martyred brother. Rather I feel complete and relieved.

****

After some years an inmate was again pulled in inside that prison cell and he found bold words of democracy on the walls all over which was written deftly and fearlessly.

We don't know what happened to Shin and where she was taken to or killed. But the words and slogans she had spread inside the walls of prison cell could illuminate the fearless Chinese who advocates for democracy and freedom. The words in Mandarin that defaced the walls are more or less translate like this.

" FREEDOM IS NECESSARY TO OUR SURVIVAL OR ELSE OUR SURVIVAL BECOMES DEFUNCT".

" RAISE YOUR FISTS TOWARD FREEDOM AND BRING AN END TO THE COMMUNIST REGIME".

" IF YOU'RE NOT AWARE OF FREEDOM THEN YOU'RE ENSLAVED AND WILL AWAYS REMAIN AS A SLAVE"

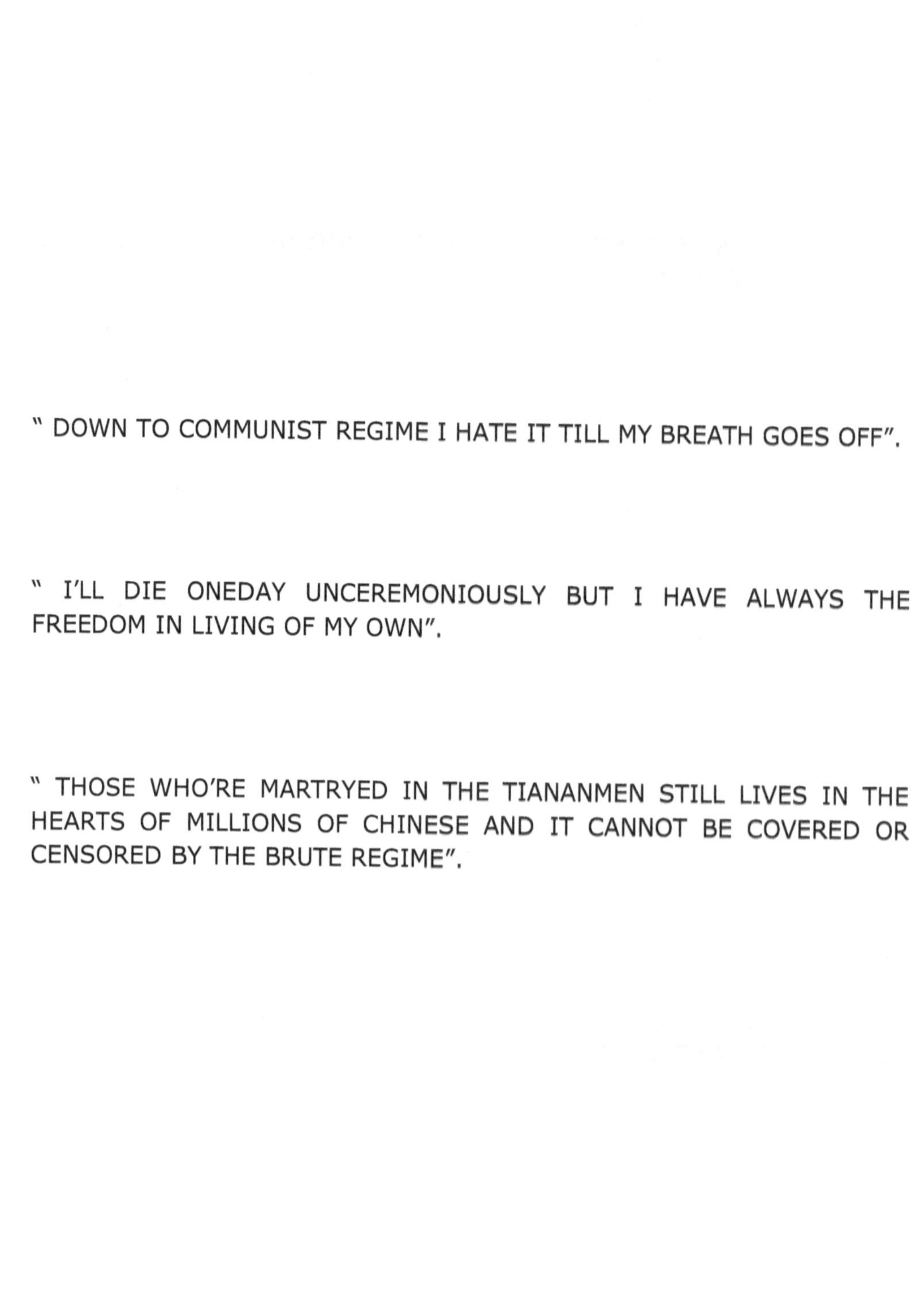

" DOWN TO COMMUNIST REGIME I HATE IT TILL MY BREATH GOES OFF".

" I'LL DIE ONEDAY UNCEREMONIOUSLY BUT I HAVE ALWAYS THE FREEDOM IN LIVING OF MY OWN".

" THOSE WHO'RE MARTRYED IN THE TIANANMEN STILL LIVES IN THE HEARTS OF MILLIONS OF CHINESE AND IT CANNOT BE COVERED OR CENSORED BY THE BRUTE REGIME".

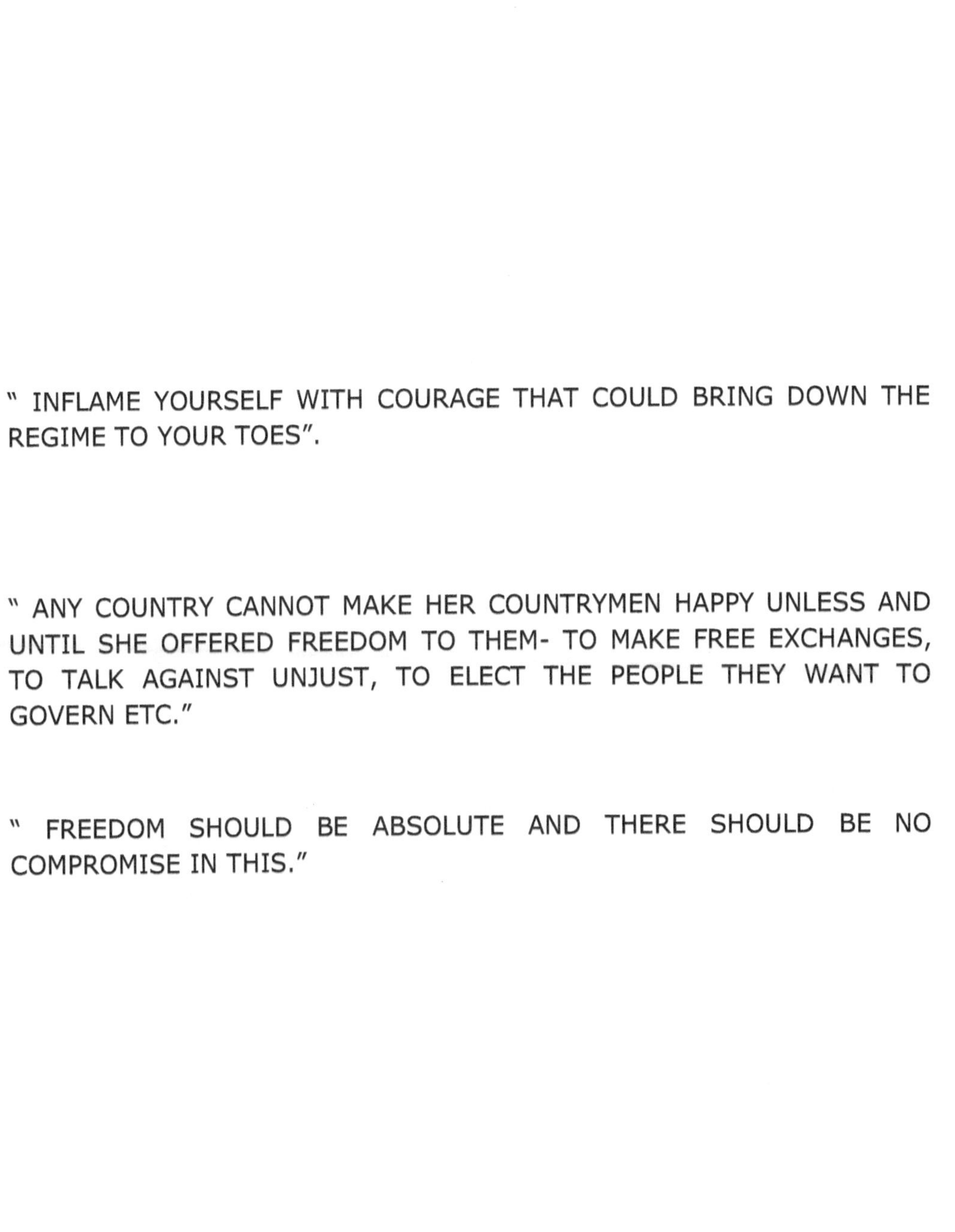

" INFLAME YOURSELF WITH COURAGE THAT COULD BRING DOWN THE REGIME TO YOUR TOES".

" ANY COUNTRY CANNOT MAKE HER COUNTRYMEN HAPPY UNLESS AND UNTIL SHE OFFERED FREEDOM TO THEM- TO MAKE FREE EXCHANGES, TO TALK AGAINST UNJUST, TO ELECT THE PEOPLE THEY WANT TO GOVERN ETC."

" FREEDOM SHOULD BE ABSOLUTE AND THERE SHOULD BE NO COMPROMISE IN THIS."

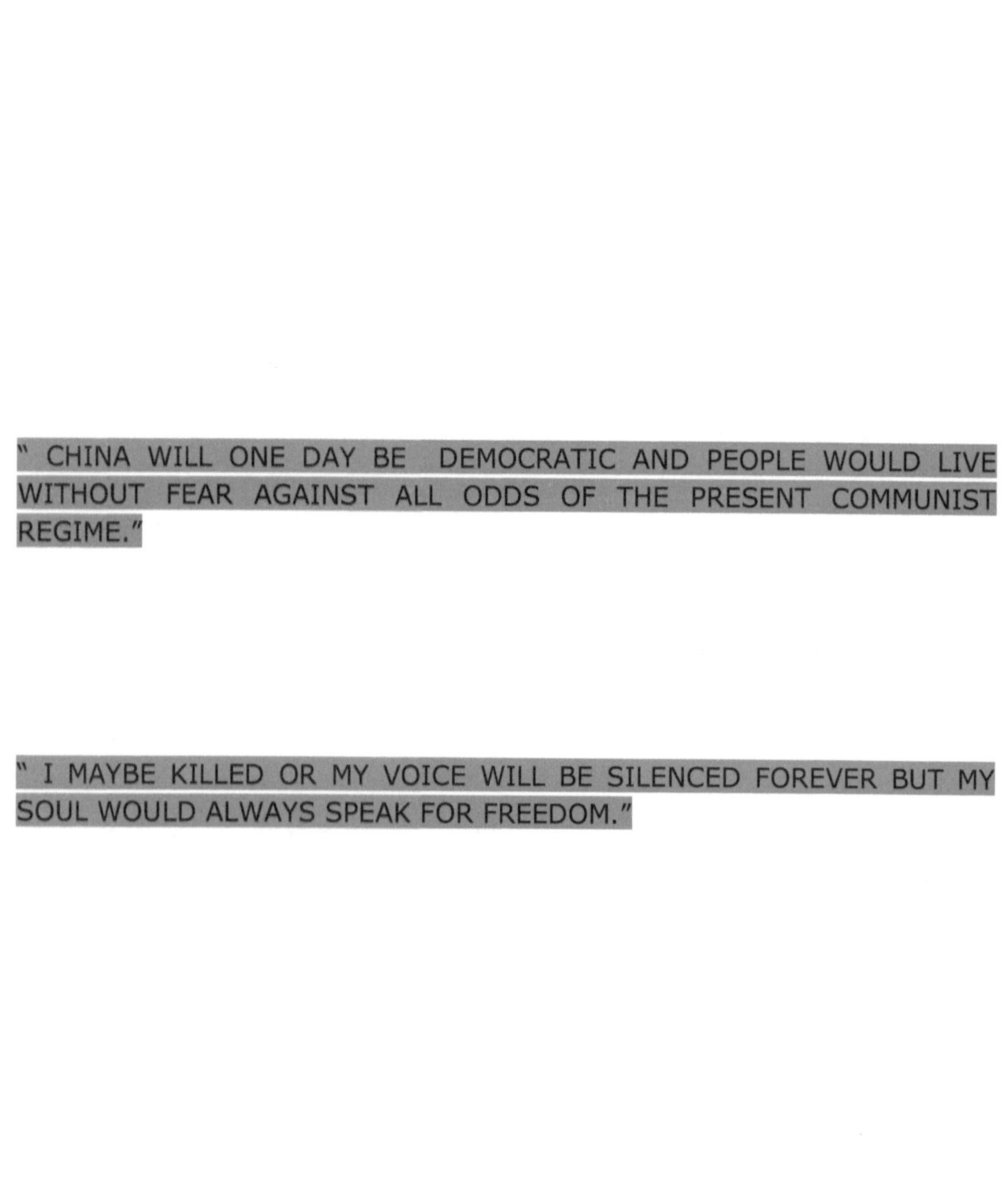
" CHINA WILL ONE DAY BE DEMOCRATIC AND PEOPLE WOULD LIVE WITHOUT FEAR AGAINST ALL ODDS OF THE PRESENT COMMUNIST REGIME."

" I MAYBE KILLED OR MY VOICE WILL BE SILENCED FOREVER BUT MY SOUL WOULD ALWAYS SPEAK FOR FREEDOM."